The Chi

A collection of gentle, pa

Penny Luker

First Published in 2021 by Bindon Books, Leyton, Cheshire, CW6 9JA
Printed by Amazon.

Acknowledgements
Many thanks to everyone who has encouraged and helped me to write this book. Thanks to LaPriel Dye for editing and proof reading. Thanks to Winsford Writers for ideas, suggestions and reading the stories; to my family for identifying points to ponder and to my husband, David, for his support.

ISBN: 9798775388584

Contents

The Child of Time

If I'd only listened to my father just a little more carefully; shown a bit more patience. I regret it now of course. Now I can no longer see him. I didn't know anything about my mother, just that she'd been beautiful and quickly bored. My father said that when mother found out she was pregnant, she didn't want to have a baby, but because he so desperately did, she'd been dutiful and careful and given him the best present that anyone ever could. As soon as she'd delivered her gift, she'd flown away. My father applied to have twenty years off work, which seemed such a long time, but of course it whirred by.

'Will you stand still for five minutes while I plait your hair?' he used to say to me when I was little.

'A little less rush and a little more care and you'll get things done more quickly,' I remember him saying.

He always had time for me. He showed me the beauty of nature and how to grow food and taught me a love of reading, which held such opportunity for learning. I was always allowed to have friends round and we travelled the world every Summer. I couldn't have asked for more.

When I was grown up, he asked me to visit him at least once a week. I'm ashamed to say that sometimes I found it a nuisance. There was so much to explore.

'I won't be here much longer. I don't have much time left,' he'd say. It wasn't a guilt trip. He knew his time was limited. In the last months I spent every minute with him. I was so scared to lose him, but he'd taught me well and there were little reminders of him all over our home.

'Don't cry for me little one. I'll always be in your heart,' he said, and so I tried to make a good life. I became an environmental scientist and spent my time monitoring endangered species and trying to put policies in place that would give them time to recover, but I was always aware that the clock was ticking. My job was my life, so I was surprised when I met Geoff, another scientist, who was as dedicated as I was to helping save creatures.

Soon we were married and I became pregnant. Deep down, I was irritated that I'd have to stop my work for a while, but then I realized what a wonderful parent I'd had, and that my baby deserved the same. How my father would've loved her, if only he'd been allowed to stay.

Within a blink of a moment, my child was grown and I was back working with Geoff on the impossible task of saving wildlife, restoring habitats and persuading people to avoid plastic, while our daughter was off at university and developing her career.

The years whizzed past. We lived every moment and became happy grandparents. I didn't understand that I'd grown old and frail. I felt full of life, with so much still to do.

Then my father returned to my side.

'I've come to help you cross over, so you won't be on your own on the journey.'

I hugged him tightly, so pleased to see him again.

'I don't want to leave Geoff, my daughter and the grandchildren. Will they be all right in this ever-changing world?'

'All of your life I've kept an eye on you. You've used your life well. It's been so lovely, as I look out for all humans to have a special human and when you've crossed over, I promise I will continue to look out for our family. Geoff will be with you soon. Be patient my child.'

'And will I meet my mother, when I cross over?'

'Good heavens, no. I thought you realised. Your mother is an eternal like me. She is the mistress of the winds. She stormed into my life like a hurricane. That's why it was so hard for her to stay still to give birth to you. Your mother has visited you on your life's journey, but never stayed for long. She knew she was not a popular visitor.'

'If both my parents are eternals, why am I an ordinary human?'

'You, my dear child are eternal in your own way. As Father Time, I instilled in you all the values I hold dear. To do that, I had to ask the powers that be, to have a brief holiday of twenty years to bring you up. Then of course, I had to return to my work. When I could, I slipped you an extra five minutes or even a year, to save some of the beautiful animals you fought for.'

'Thank you, father, but that doesn't explain why I'm not an eternal.'

'I don't know how to say this delicately, so I'll just come out with it. The powers that be, have to give permission for eternals to have children, but when I saw your mother, I was completely bowled over by her. We couldn't help ourselves. They accepted there was no malice on our part and so permitted us to become your parents. They understood your mother couldn't stay in one place for long, so granted me a short break of twenty years.'

'How many other children have you had?' I asked.

'You're my only child. That's why they let me bring you up. It cost them a lot because they had to step in and do all the jobs that I usually do.'

'Just now you said I was eternal in my own way. What did you mean?'

'I meant that you'll live on in your children, and your children's children, and although you'll not meet them until they cross over, I will call by whenever I can and tell you all their news.'

‘I’m glad I’ll be able to see you now and again. Is it time?’

‘Yes, my child. Give me your hand.’

And we walked together, Father Time and the child who should never have been, slowly up the stairs and for the first time, I felt that time was no longer ticking. It was meandering like a river.

Hidden

Gerald trampled through the sand dunes carrying his digging equipment and packed lunch. It was a warm day with a gentle breeze and he was looking forward to excavating the isolated plot he'd thought as being 'of interest' from his bi-plane.

He'd not been able to identify the shrubs growing over the small piece of land, and now that he could touch them and smell their slightly acrid aroma, he was none the wiser. He'd take a bit home with him later, to see what he could make of it. Callously, he ripped it all out of the ground. It came away easily, as the roots were shallow. It was strange it just grew in this one place, as if it had been imported from another land.

He started to dig. He marked out a rectangle with string and pegs and thrust the shovel into the dry, sandy earth. Although the top few inches were easy to move, being little more than dust, the next level was solid and hard, but he was a strong man, even if he was past his prime. As the day grew warmer, he dug on, shovel after shovel full of earth. Slowly, he was disappearing into the hole because the earth was piling up around the edge, but he didn't mind. It was pleasant listening to the distant sound of the waves lapping on the shore. They were calming, almost a melody.

Suddenly, he came across a white bone. He knew now that he'd not found an ancient site of waste disposal, where he might find treasures, but a burial site. That was fine. Sometimes people were buried with treasures or artefacts of value. He might still be lucky. He also knew that now he must dig with extreme care, so as not to damage the skeleton. He climbed out of the excavation to get his other tools and decided it was time to drink the warm tea in his flask. It was easy to forget the physical strain when doing such manual work. The tea tasted delicious and he was tempted to rest in the sun, listening to the sea, but there was a lot of work still to be done, so he pressed on.

With care, he meticulously removed earth, while trying to leave the bones lying in the same position. He would stop in a minute to take a photograph, because it was important to record the progress of a find.

Once again, he climbed out, this time to retrieve his camera. The brightness of the sun shocked him, but then he'd been working in the shade, totally concentrating on not damaging the skeleton. He looked down to take a photograph and couldn't believe his eyes. The skeleton he'd unearthed was like none he'd ever seen. In fact, it was incredible. Adrenaline surged through his body. He couldn't remember ever feeling so excited. Carefully, he climbed back down and removed more of the red earth. The lower half of the skeleton was particularly delicate.

At regular intervals he poked his head up and checked no-one was watching. This find would make him rich. His friends, if you could call them that, would stop laughing at his 'little hobby'. He'd be world famous. Gerald Farthing, archaeologist extraordinaire; finder of the unique skeleton. He could see himself being invited to universities to explain why he'd decided to dig there. He must remember to collect a sample of that shrub he'd pulled up. In his mind he was almost writing the speech he would make. He would start with his solo flight over the area...

He was so engrossed with his musings that he failed to register the gentle rhythm of the waves had evolved into delicate Gaelic music, which was seeping into his head. The music was exquisite, hauntingly hypnotic, even spiritual. It lulled him from consciousness to a state of euphoria.

Gently, he started to caress the smooth, pure white bones. They felt like silk to his roughened hands. They were so beautiful, like a work of art. The music intoxicated him, until his eyes closed and he lay down, curling his body around the skeleton.

Gradually, the hole he'd spent the day digging, started to fill itself in, piling deeper and deeper over him. The mud tumbled, like water going down a drain, with a force too great to fight against. The unknown shrub was pulled back on top of the grave and the plot looked as if no-one had been there.

With his last ounce of strength, Gerald held his camera up, in the hope that someone would see it. He cursed himself for not recognizing what extreme danger he was in. He should have realized, when he'd discovered the pure white bones of a mermaid.

The Soul Takers

Long ago, in the times of gods and myths, lived Hades. He was the god of the underworld and by default had a terrible reputation. When people died, their souls were sent to the underworld in ancient carriages that could travel across land or water.

When the souls of the dead arrived, Hades, sometimes helped by his wife, Persephone, had to make sure the souls were sent to the appropriate place. Sometimes the souls had lived a good and honourable life and they could live comfortably in the underworld until they were ready to rest in peace.

Others had tried to lead good lives, but needed to pay penance for some wrongdoing on their part. Only then could they rest.

But there were some souls that were evil and had caused havoc and pain for most of their lives. They had to be kept separate from the other souls, as they were always ready to corrupt others, and had no sense of guilt or regret.

This last group were extremely difficult to deal with, and as time went by, Hades had to become sterner and more fierce in how he dealt with them.

The screams from the dark corner grew so loud and penetrating that Persephone had to escape from the underground world to strengthen her energy levels, but she loved Hades and always returned.

More and more souls were sent to the underworld and Hades grew tired; not because he was lazy but because he was so overworked.

'Come husband dear,' said Persephone, 'you need to appoint a manager to run the dark corner and an assistant to help you sort the souls.'

Hades heeded his wife's words. First, he asked the gods if they could help him, but none wanted to live in the underworld, so then he set about finding two honourable men. After many months, he found Aaron and Abbe.

Aaron was a strong man, who had high moral values and a good heart. He appointed him the manager of the dark corner. Abbe was an honourable man and he was offered the job to work beside Hades, sorting souls.

The years passed and many in the dark corner tried to bully or manipulate Aaron, to let them travel back across the river, and be alive again, but Aaron resisted the temptation. Abbe worked quietly alongside Hades and learned how to read souls. All was well in the underworld and Hades was able to relax a little.

Then one day, the carriage arrived and the most dreadful souls were sorted and sent to the dark corner. They told Aaron that his wife had forgotten who he was, and suggested he take the carriage back to visit her. Aaron researched if this was possible. He knew he was dead and that his place was in the underworld, but he needed to see his wife, just one more time.

'You're right he told the latest group of souls. We will visit my wife for just one night and to cover our absence we'll need to take a soul back with us from the living. You can be my guards.'

'So, if we stayed away two nights, we'd need to take back two souls,' asked one of the dark souls.

'That's right, but we'll only stay one night. We cannot cheat death.'

The carriage was prepared, the lantern lit and Aaron and a group of twenty souls left the underworld, while Hades slept.

As they crossed the River Styx, the sky grew dark and the wind howled. The candle blew out, but Aaron kept to his path to go and see his wife. When it was nearly morning, he realized that the souls he'd taken along to guard him, had gone, and he knew what a terrible thing he'd done. He'd betrayed his master and must head straight back to face his punishment, without seeing his wife.

Abbe, became aware that all was not right with the underworld. He went to find Hades, but found Persephone reading a book about nature.

Abbe explained that those who should be in the dark corner, would run around the world stealing souls, so that they didn't have to return to the underworld. This would leave mankind in a dark place. Eventually all the human race would lose ambition, ingenuity, hope and happiness.

'Leave Hades to sleep, Abbe. Carry on with your good work, as you have always done. I'll deal with this.'

When Hades woke up and found out what Aaron had done, he roared with a thunder that frightened the whole underworld, but when he looked into Aaron's heart, he knew him to be truly sorry, and recognized he had returned to face his punishment, without seeing his wife. He put his arm around him.

'You're still a good man, Aaron. I put you in with the worst souls that ever there were, and I should've supported you more. You've served for many years as a loyal servant. We'll find you an assistant, so you too can have some rest.

Meanwhile, Persephone took her white carriage and filled it with seeds and bulbs and set off on her journey. To this day, she chases around the world to seek all those that are lost, and she replenishes their lives with beauty, colour and love and with each spring flower a desperate soul is healed. And every Autumn she brings back one of the escaped souls and returns them to the dark corner.

A Night to Remember

Storm could feel that the house was bitterly cold, which wasn't surprising as it was November, tomorrow. She had nowhere else to go. She shivered. The silence seemed to be holding its breath. Dumping her bags on to the over-patterned carpet, she flicked the light switch, but nothing happened, so she went in search of the fuse box.

Her Great Aunt had left her the house and the solicitor had sent her the keys. She hadn't been going to move straight in but her mother's new boyfriend, Jim, had been quite threatening this morning and it seemed the safest thing to do was to move out quickly. The journey hadn't been too long but she could only bring as much as she could carry.

What was that noise? There was a thin screeching yelping sound. She must be imagining things.

Once the lights were working, she went to the kitchen to see if a cup of tea would lift her spirits. The water seemed to struggle from the tap protesting and making a knocking sound. She looked around and found the kettle and heard a scuttling of tiny feet. But she could see no sign of mice. Storm was glad she was still wearing tall boots with her jeans tucked into them. Her phone rang.

'What's the point of leaving if you leave all your rotten stuff here?' shouted Jim.

'I couldn't carry it,' Storm replied. 'I've packed it all up and I'll come back a couple of times tomorrow and pick it up.'

'No, you won't, I'll bring it to you now,' said Jim and the phone went dead.

Rubbing her arms to try to get warmer she looked around the old-fashioned kitchen. It needed a good clean, but that was a job for tomorrow. She took her tea and started to climb the stairs. When she'd nearly reached the top, she glanced through the banisters and saw a door close. Somebody was in the house!

She thought quickly. If she left the house, she'd be out in the night with nowhere to go. She'd have to investigate. Slowly, she climbed the last few stairs. She opened the door. She could hear the blood rushing round her head. Flicking the light switch, the room looked empty, and searching under the bed, in the cupboards revealed nothing.

Storm heard the thin screech again.

'Who's there?' she called out, but there was no reply. Quickly, she searched the other rooms and then finding nothing, she sat down on one of the beds. At first, she thought she was seeing things as smoky images of four teenagers wafted away from the wall, but as she looked more closely, they became more solid looking. Her heart was thumping and she couldn't move. She tried to speak but no words came out.

'You've gate crashed our party,' said the tallest being. 'If you want to leave, we'll let you go. NOW.'

She nodded. 'I haven't got anywhere I can go,' she muttered, but she stood up and was sidling past them when there was a loud banging on the door.

'Well, you'd better answer it,' said the tall ghost. 'We can't.' Then he laughed his shrill laugh and Storm shivered.

She ran downstairs and threw open the door.

'So, this is where you're hiding out,' Jim said, walking into the house with two large bin liners. Not a bad place; much nicer than I expected. You all on your own?'

'Not exactly,' she muttered.

'Oh, but I think you are. I quite fancy having a mother and daughter,' he said, as he grabbed her and pushed her into the main living room.

'If you touch me, I'll tell mother and then you'll be out on your ear. Do you want to risk that?' she shouted.

'Ohhh, you'll tell mummy, will you? I doubt if she'll believe you, will she? She hasn't believed any of the other poison you've been telling her about me, has she?'

She could feel his grip digging into her arms and then she felt his breath on her face. Just at that moment, she heard the shrill, yelping sound. It grew louder as it came nearer and nearer. She saw a brief look of terror in Jim's eyes and then blackness closed over her like a protective cloak and she knew no more.

When she woke, it was morning. She was lying on the carpet with her head resting on her tapestry bag and her sleeping bag had been pulled over her. There was no sign of Jim, and as she was fully clothed, she felt sure he hadn't done anything to her. She called to the ghosts, but there was no sign of them anywhere. There was no response.

Storm made herself a cup of tea and pondered over the previous night's events. She certainly hadn't imagined Jim, because there were her bags in the hall. She couldn't have imagined the ghosts either, or Jim wouldn't have left. They'd saved her. She'd spoilt their party, but they'd stopped her being hurt. Lifted by this thought she set about cleaning the house. She put the heating on and scrubbed and polished until the place looked spotless. As she went along, she packed away most of her Great Aunt's knick knacks and some of the furniture into the smallest bedroom. Soon her new home was looking a lot less cluttered. When she finished, it was evening and she went to the main room and sat on the bed.

'I don't know whether you can hear me, but I want to say 'Thank You' for saving me. Surely, we could share the house.'

She waited and waited but there was no reply, but then she noticed a smoky form emerging from the wallpaper. It was the tallest ghost. As he started to take a more solid form, she heard him speak.

'I had to get special permission to talk to you tonight. We only come back to earth on one night of the year. We should've listened to you, when you said you'd no place to go. We chased the man off and stayed with you until we had to leave. I'm glad you're all right.'

'You didn't get much of a party then?'

'No, but for the first time in years, we actually helped someone and that felt fantastic.'

'I'll always be grateful. In fact, come back next year and I'll leave the house empty for the night and you can have your party.'

'No, stay in next year and we'll pop in and say hello. We might see if we can work out a way to help someone else. I have to go.'

'What's your name,' she called as his image faded.

'Thomas Driver,' whispered a faint voice as he disappeared.

'Tomorrow, I'm going to find out all about you, Thomas Driver,' she thought.

Then her phone went. It was her mother.

'What did you do to poor Jim last night? He's been a jabbering wreck all day. I want to know what went on.'

Storm paused. What was the point in saying anything to her mother? Jim was right; she wouldn't be believed.

'Nothing of any substance happened while he was here mum. He met a few of my friends. It was so useful that he brought all my clobber round. Saved me a lot of time today.'

When she put the phone down, she smiled to herself. She had a safe place to live and she hadn't even lied to her mother.

The Eclipse

I didn't know why he'd brought me to this place at this time. The light was eerie. I can't really describe it; like some of the colour had been sucked out. It's always a bit chilly in the forest, but today it seemed worse. I could smell the rotting leaves and damp earth. Carl, my step-father, had dropped me and my dog, Barnie at the side of the forest, but something had freaked Barnie and he'd run off.

The sky became gradually darker, but what surprised me was the birds stopped singing and soon there was no sound at all. I wished Barnie was with me. Where had he got too? I hoped he was all right.

I wished I wasn't so alone. For some reason I thought of the story of Hansel and Gretal and then I remembered that Carl had given me instructions to find and collect charcoal burner mushrooms for our tea. In my pocket I had a photocopy of the mushroom. Suddenly I remembered that he and Mum didn't like mushrooms. Why would he want me to collect them? He'd let me take Barnie to the forest because I said I wouldn't go on my own but where had Barnie gone? The sky went completely dark.

It occurred to me that Carl must have known the sun would disappear. He was trying to scare me. I'd been told about the eclipse at school, but had forgotten when it was going to happen.

I decided that I'd be safer if I got out of this part of the forest. Perhaps I could get back to the road and hitch a lift to my aunt's house. After what seemed like hours, but was probably only a few minutes, I began to see dim outlines. As I stumbled along, I looked up and there saw Barnie hanging from a tree. I'd known that Barnie wouldn't leave me and I knew this was a trap. If I went to rescue him, Carl would probably hurt me. He was always saying what a waste of money I was; an uncontrollable, spoilt child. He used to whisper how weird I was to believe in the supernatural and I'd be better off dead. He'd been nice to me, until mum had married him, and he was still nice in front of her, but sometimes he looked at me with such coldness in his eyes. I didn't know why. Just because I was a little different. He only had to wait a few years and I'd be able to leave home. I really did hate him. I wished he were dead. At that moment a stray beam of light showed a path to Barnie. It was unearthly.

I couldn't leave Barnie struggling. I took out my knife. My stepfather could be anywhere in the moving shadows. I'd just have to be quick. I took a deep breath and ran towards Barnie, slashed at his lead which was looped onto the branch and caught him in my left arm. I felt a movement behind me and ran forwards, dropping Barnie to the ground. He ran with me, crashing through leaves and twigs, while I still clutched the knife in my hand. It was a hard slog, with the ground being bumpy and tree roots adding to the hazardousness of the route. The light was creeping back. I looked behind me. There was no-one there.

When we reached the road, we made our way to the bus stop. It wasn't that far. I couldn't see Carl's car, so maybe he wasn't in the woods. I decided to phone home.

'Hi Mum. Is Carl with you?'

'You haven't lost him, have you? He thought it'd be so nice to go and watch the eclipse with you. A bonding exercise.'

I knew there was no point in arguing with her. Carl definitely hadn't asked me to go and watch the eclipse.

'Did you want us to get you some mushrooms?' I asked.

'Don't be daft. You know we don't like them. Why would you ask that?'

I said good-bye as the bus came and I lifted Barnie up the steep step.

'Keep him off the seats,' mumbled the bus driver.

As I sat down with Barnie on to my lap, I noticed Carl's car, tucked away just off the road, so he was in the forest.

Carl didn't come home. He was found later that night. He'd tripped in the forest and fallen on his own knife. I felt a little guilty. I'd wished him dead and now he was. It was just at the turning point of the eclipse. There'd been that strange shaft of light. Had I unwittingly called on powers from beyond, that I didn't understand?

Mother knows best

'You know I'm not a restrictive mother, Lucinda. I let you have a lot of freedom. I just don't want you to go out this evening.'

'And you know, I love you Mum, but I've promised to go to the pictures with Martha. I can't let her down.'

'I've had this premonition that something awful is going to happen and I'll never see you again. I've had this feeling of doom all day.'

'Mum, you're always having premonitions and they virtually never come true. Love you. Must go,' Lucinda said as the door slammed behind her.

She'd known to go quickly. These anxiety attacks of her mum's, just kept getting worse and she wouldn't go and get help.

Lucinda was sauntering down the road as she was going to be a bit early, although they had booked seats, so she could actually go in and sit in comfort. She texted Martha and speeded up her journey.

It seemed the world and its mother had the same idea. The place was packed. She hunkered down with her giant bag of Maltesers and Coke and soon Martha arrived. They chattered throughout the adverts and were just settling down for the main feature, when the floor shook and there was a loud explosion. Lucinda immediately looked towards Martha, but she wasn't there. She called her name as loudly as she could but there was no sign. It was difficult to see in the dark and smoke further hindered her vision. There was a sharp smell, that made her eyes water. She knew she needed to get out of the building in case there was another explosion. Feeling her way along the row she made it to the end and then to the stairs.

Intent on getting out quickly, Lucinda almost missed the small child, covered in dirt with tear splodges all down her face, sitting in the wide corridor.

'Where's mummy?' she asked quickly.

'Mummy's gone,' the child wailed.

She made a quick decision, believing the child to be in danger, and scooped her up and continued running. As she turned the corner, a young man stood there with a device that looked like a bomb. He had a cord he was about to pull.

'Let the child go through. Whatever you're fighting for, let this innocent live. She's hurt nobody,' she shouted, although she couldn't hear her own voice.

He leaned towards her threateningly and screamed at her, 'RUN'. She read his lips.

Lucinda didn't need asking twice. With the child in her arms, she ran as fast as she could. Very few people made it out of the cinema, but Lucinda made it to safety and handed the child over to the ambulance crew, who arrived in the road within minutes.

Once she'd been checked over and given her details to a policewoman, she was allowed to go.

The 'terrorist' turned out to be a local teenager, who'd been rejected by his peers and ridiculed for his stutter. He'd known many of his classmates were going to be at the cinema. He didn't make it out alive, but it turned out later, he'd had a small sister.

The cool, clear night sky and gentle drizzle were welcome refreshment to Lucinda, but she didn't dawdle. She knew if her mum switched on the news then she'd be worrying.

As she opened the door, the house was completely quiet. She found her mum sitting on the sofa, with a large glass of vodka and an empty bottle of pills, by her side. Her skin was cold. Her mother's prediction had come true. When she'd left the house that evening it was the last time her mother saw her.

What Goes Around

Wayne woke up to whiteness. It was so bright that he could hardly see. His head felt as if a sledge hammer had landed right across his temple. Half-heartedly he looked round for his twin.

'Where the smeg is this?' he muttered. Then he closed his eyes again to shut out the piercing light. He tried to sit up, but a wave of nausea swept over him and he sank back to the hard floor. He called out.

'Bruce, where the frigging hell are you?'

He heard a groan to his left. Slowly he lifted his head and reached out his hand. He touched a sticky, soft woven material. He retracted his hand automatically.

Wayne peered again through the whiteness and saw the shape of Bruce lying on his side, wearing a kind of silver coloured netting. At that moment Bruce started retching and vomited all over the floor. The smell reached Wayne and threatened to overwhelm him, but a white pipe swung out from the wall and sucked the floor clean. A smell of pine slowly permeated the air. His brother groaned.

Time passed and gradually Wayne and Bruce woke up properly; their eyes adjusting to the light. They found they were in a pod. It was not high enough for them to stand up in, but it still felt roomy. They started to search for a doorway, but could find none.

'Where's our smegging clothes gone?' asked Bruce, 'and why are we wrapped in this sticky web stuff? It ain't frigging right.'

'I don't know bruv. Last I remember we was leaving The George. Who would've taken our clothes and wrapped us up like this? It's probably some sorta joke.'

There was a high pitched noise and a giant eye appeared on one of the walls. Bruce grabbed hold of Wayne and they both retreated to the back of the pod. Their gaze was fixed upon the eye. As their vision became clearer, they could see that the eye was behind the wall, which had become transparent. The large eye was situated in a furry head and eight hairy legs were waving up and down. A deep voice vibrated through the air.

'Welcome Wayne and Bruce. You are wondering why you are here. Let me explain.'

Wayne felt a rush of warmth against his leg and realized Bruce had just wet himself and covered the floor, once again. The white pipe swung out from the wall for a second time and cleaned them both up. A fresh smell of pine wafted through the pod.

'As I was saying, normally we just watch and collect information when we visit your planet. We don't interfere with humans as it might change the data, but you two were so terribly poisoned with alcohol, you would've died, so we picked you up and brought you to planet Arachnid. Here we've kept you safe from all pollutants and from our atmosphere, which would kill you within seconds. Most of the poison has now been emitted from your bodies and we are working on bringing you some food. The air we have piped in will keep you healthy.'

'What will happen to us? How long will you keep us here?' asked Wayne.

'We will take you back to Earth as soon as you are fully well. This is our gift to you. A debt repaid. Ah here is your food. Enjoy.'

A little hatch opened and two plates of salad and two glasses of water were placed on the floor beside them.

'What the...' Bruce started to say.

'Shut the smeg up. Eat the food. We're prisoners and we don't need to annoy the hairy eye now, do we?'

Both boys looked at each other and then quietly ate their salads. Time passed. Wayne and Bruce didn't know how much time. There was no night and day, just whiteness. Salad and water were served for every meal. To pass the time they started to pick off the web that encased them. It was strangely satisfying, like bursting bubble wrap. As they picked it off they talked about what they could remember that night at The George, and of all the things they hadn't done in their lives, and wanted to do.

'The furry eye is right you know,' said Bruce. 'We really did overdo the drink. I can't remember how much I downed, and if I'm honest it's not much fun going out on a Saturday and getting so wasted, that you feel like death all Sunday.'

'I don't even know how we started doing it. I suppose we should really use our lives for good - if we ever get home,' said Wayne.

'What d'you mean if? I want to travel to Australia and see all the wildlife and animals there. It'd be great to be able to work my way around the world,' said Bruce.

'I think you'd learn a lot doing that and you could take photos and build a portfolio. I've always wanted to go to university and study science and become a vet. Yes bruv, if we get out of here alive, we should vow to make more of our lives.'

At last they had picked off all the webbing and within seconds the hairy eye appeared. Wayne and Bruce shrank back to the furthest wall.

'Now you're ready to go home. When you were young Wayne, you showed kindness to one of us. You stopped a cruel child, named Gerald, from pulling off our legs. Now we have said thank you. We've made your sick bodies healthy. We've given your pickled brains a chance to recover. All the signs are good but we won't rescue you again. Your clothes will be delivered and then we'll take you home.'

Bruce's face looked pale but Wayne realized that he was feeling well for the first time in years. They had been stupid to follow the self-destructing actions of some so-called friends.

'Thank you for helping us,' said Wayne. 'We won't waste our lives from now on.'

The next thing they knew they woke up and found they were laying on their bedroom floor. They looked at each other, but decided they couldn't speak about their ordeal. After all, who would believe them? Later that week they began to doubt themselves whether any of it was real, but Wayne started applying to universities and Bruce began planning his world travel. They both wanted to make a difference and maybe the spiders were watching.

The Magic Quest

Lady Viviane quickly braided her hair into a single plait and then slipped on her cotton tunic. She laced up both sides of a short leather over-garment and then struggled into the light chainmail suit that she'd had specially made. The fine links were almost the quality of jewellery and clung to her body, emphasizing her beauty. The King's Knights would deride her chainmail as ineffective and think she had chosen something different because of female vanity, but it was far from that. Her strength was her nimbleness and suppleness. Ordinary chainmail would have made it impossible to move at speed and would have worn her out. In the quiet of her cold, isolated rooms she'd reinforced her suit with magic. Her armour was now as strong as any other knight's and maybe stronger, but magic was not practised openly in Jarvert. Few had the gift and it was often treated with suspicion.

King Rufus had laughed outright at her request to become a Knight of Jarvert and set her, what he thought, was an impossible task. He'd given her two weeks to train and prepare for a contest with Gawain, one of his fiercest and most skilled knights. Lady Viviane picked up her handcrafted sword, made to suit her slight, sinuous frame and headed for the castle's practice grounds.

'Now, child, if you want to withdraw from the contest, no-one will think less of you for it. It's hardly a womanly pursuit to fight, and definitely not for a lady of noble blood,' Rufus said in a fatherly tone, although he was only slightly older than herself.

Kazar caught her eye and gave a pleading stare, but she turned away from him. Being a knight was the only way she would spend time with Kazar, as he accompanied Rufus on the many trips to push back the Charlons. She longed for Kazar in a way that only the two of them knew. That he was older didn't matter to her. She craved his touch, but most of all she was determined to learn more of his magic.

'No, Sire! I asked for this chance and I'm ready. My noble blood is now just a dream, as both my father and his lands are gone. I am your loyal subject, Sire and wish to serve you, by fighting the Charlons.'

'Noble blood is not deleted by the loss of your lands, Lady Viviane, but I promised you the opportunity, and if you insist, let the contest commence. Gawain, my friend, try not to harm Lady Viviane overmuch.'

Gawain saluted King Rufus and made himself ready. Kazar prepared to intervene with magic if he needed to and Rufus settled down to watch.

'I wish you success, Lady Viviane. You represent the women of Jarvert,' Queen Eleanor said and smiled serenely.

The contest started. Gawain raised his sword towards Lady Viviane, but each time he aimed for her sword, she ducked and danced. Rufus laughed out loud. Then their swords met. The crowd hushed. Gawain was strong. The smaller sword must fall, but it didn't. Gawain raised his game. He moved more quickly and put more force into the swipes and charges. Suddenly he was beating her. She was retreating. He relaxed, ready for the surrender. Then she was pushing him back. On and on she came. Queen Eleanor stood on her feet and shouted.

'Come on, Lady Viviane. Come on.'

Rufus raised an eyebrow at his wife and she sat down.

Gawain exerted more effort and his sword clashed and sent Lady Viviane's sword flying. He'd won. He smiled and then she dived and rolled and when she was standing again, the sword was back in her hand. Kazar looked on helplessly, just relieved that she was still alive. The swords met and parted as she danced and dived and then Gawain tripped and fell. Lady Viviane quickly aimed her sword at his throat and held it there.

'Do you surrender, Gawain?'

'I tripped.'

'Do you surrender?'

Gawain looked at Rufus, who nodded. The smile had gone from Rufus's face and Queen Eleanor lowered her eyes, but a little smile hovered on her lips.

'Yes I surrender, Lady Viviane. You are indeed a good fighter.' He stood up and brushed himself off.

'Knights, Kazar, we will meet in the main hall, now. Lady Viviane please join us after our meal.'

Rufus strode off and his knights followed. Kazar smiled reassuringly at Lady Viviane. She smiled back. She'd done it. She'd fought a knight and won. Quickly she made her way to her rooms and changed into a plain deep blue robe, edged with lace. She carefully placed her chainmail and sword in a trunk and locked it with both a key and magic.

When Lady Viviane arrived at the main hall, she was asked to come in, but not invited to sit down.

'I promised you the opportunity to try to become a knight and you have acquitted yourself well, however I cannot make you a knight. You're a woman. Our enemies would take it as a sign of desperation. It would be an invitation to attack Jarvert. I cannot put Jarvert at risk, although it grieves me to break my word to you. Instead you will have a reward. You may marry any knight of your choice.'

Lady Viviane faced Rufus head on. 'I thought you were man of honour. I don't want to marry any of your knights. I wanted...'

'Sire, may I suggest an alternative solution?' said Kazar.

'Oh, what other solution is there Kazar?' he said in a voice, betraying irritation. Then he looked at his old friend and took a deep breath. 'Go on Kazar.'

'I've watched Lady Viviane handle horses. She has a rare talent. She can calm them when they're distressed and heal them when they're hurt. I've known her walk them into the lake and tame their fury in such a gentle way. You could offer her the position of Carer of the Knights' mounts. Then she could ride with the knights on our missions. Being a carer of animals would be an acceptable job for a woman. She could be given permission to wear her armour and sword as they are nothing like the real thing but would offer her some status and protection.'

Rufus looked round the table and the other Knights nodded.

'Lady Viviane, ignoring your earlier comment about my honour, which I'm sure you didn't mean, would you accept the position of Carer of the Knights' mounts?' said Rufus.

'Oh yes, Sire. I'd be deeply honoured. Thank you Kazar for your suggestion,' she smiled.

'Yes, thank you Kazar,' said Rufus. He looked at the Lady and then at Kazar. 'Don't you two come from the same place? Is that where you've seen her talent with horses?'

'Yes, Sire. We're both from Cazer-Foriddin. I was her teacher for a while,' said Kazar.

'A place I must visit sometime, as it's produced such gifted people.' Rufus waved his hand at them and the meeting ended. Everyone left the main hall.

On her way to her rooms, at the other end of the castle, Lady Viviane was passed by a lady in deep purple, flowing robes. The lady mirrored her own beauty. She inclined her head, but the woman swept by, without acknowledging her. It was only as she reached her rooms, she realized the woman was Iseult, a powerful sorcerer, who'd proclaimed herself as Rufus's enemy. Lady Viviane opened the shutter and leaned out of the narrow slit in the castle wall. She hurled magic at the warning bell and set it ringing. Quickly, she ran to find Kazar. Only he had magic that might be powerful enough to defeat Iseult, but he might be in danger. She drew her magic to her, ready to join forces with Kazar if needed. Kazar was her destiny and only he could help her develop her magic for the dangerous tasks she knew lay ahead.

Winter Spirit

Her first thought, when she awoke from the long sleep, was for her son. She was sure he was in danger. He was nearly eighteen and due to inherit his trust fund. Shirley knew she must get to him quickly and warn him. She looked around her. Snow lay on the ground three inches deep, on the late October evening, but she wasn't cold. An old man kicked a ball against the side of a gravestone. Perhaps he looked a little bored, but he glanced her way and nodded. He seemed affable enough and the fear from the strangeness of her surroundings ebbed. The light from the moon cast a silvery glow, which made everyone seem ethereal. She laughed silently to herself.

Most people were heading for the lych gate, so she followed the increasing crowd, leaving the man pounding his ball against the solid marble headstone.

Shirley wandered down the hill away from the church and through the village, past the shops and the school, to the quiet lane where she lived. It was chocolate box pretty, with the white covered houses and trees. The large Georgian house that had once been her home, had lights blazing, seemed to be calling her onwards.

As she drew closer, she could see the light came from downstairs, which suggested that Gerald was still up. She automatically went to the front door but of course it was shut. What could she do? She wasn't sure she could do a knock on the door any more. Creeping quietly up to the window she peeped inside. There he was sitting asleep in the armchair, with his mouth open and his legs splayed. On the nearby table was a tumbler of the whisky he loved so much. It seemed as though nothing had changed, but how was she going to get in? She looked down at her clothes. The pale blue silk pyjamas were what she'd been wearing the last time she saw him, not her best dress that they'd placed on her for the long sleep. The rules of death were not yet clear to her, but she was glad not to be wearing what he'd chosen. So, could living spirits walk through glass, she wondered? Now was the time to find out. She drew herself up to her full height, gathered her courage and walked straight through the window. She'd expected to feel some resistance, or some sensation of substance, but there was none. Her mood lifted a little but she knew she must reach her son. An image of the old man from the graveyard, kicking the ball, with the timing of an old grandfather clock, flashed through her mind.

She made her way upstairs and found her son, Robert, fast asleep on his bed. The room was its usual mess – a sort of organised chaos. His guitar was carefully propped up by a chair and there were clothes spilling over from the laundry basket. The only difference she could see, was a picture of herself, stuck to the wall with blue-tac. Shirley watched him as he slept and all the love she felt for him surged through her. Death didn't kill love, she thought. That was good to know. Suddenly, his eyes sprang open and he sat up with a start.

With a quickness of youth, that she envied, he spoke.

'Mum, I've so missed you. Is it you? How did you get here?'

'Oh, I've missed you too my darling Robert, but I have a feeling that we haven't much time. I've come to warn you. I think you're in danger. I don't know exactly how he did it, but your stepfather poisoned me. I thought he loved me, but he just wanted our money. On your birthday, you'll inherit some money from me and he'll want it, if he hasn't already spent it. You must leave.'

'What old Gerald, I'm sure I can handle him, although, now you mention it, he's getting me to sign some papers tomorrow. He said it's so the trust fund can be transferred to me.'

'Robert, you must leave now. If you don't sign, we don't know what might happen.'

Robert looked thoughtful. 'I wondered why we weren't using a solicitor.'

He threw his legs out of bed and stood up towering over Shirley. 'I wish I could hug you,' he said, 'but you're looking a bit translucent.'

'You know I would give you a bear hug if I could, but we mustn't waste time. Please pack a bag and go to your Aunt Cathy. She'll look after you. Will you do that for me?'

Robert looked a bit exasperated, but he picked up a back pack and started loading clothes, both clean and dirty into it.

'I'll go to Dad's. I'm seeing a lot more of him these days. He's really sorry, well, about... you. And he's made it clear that he wants to be in my life and be there for me. I'll be safe there.'

Shirley thought about his dad. There was still a little part of her that loved him, even after he'd gone off with the glamorous Gloria, from Finance. She looked a little less glamorous nowadays, with two children under three, Shirley thought, surprised she could still feel bitchy about her. She liked the fact that even now she was still herself. Yes, Robert would be safe there. His dad would look out for him.

'Good idea. I'd say send him my love, but he'd think you were mad.' She smiled and Robert gave her his lop-sided grin. 'Now we must be quiet going out or we'll wake Gerald.'

'No need to worry about that. He's drinking really heavily these days. He never wakes up until about four in the morning. I hear him banging up the stairs to go to bed.'

Robert put the bag on his back, adjusted it, picked up his precious guitar and they started down the stairs. As they were going past the living room, where loud snores were emanating, Robert whispered, 'What poison did he use to kill you?'

'He used my heart pills. He must've ground them up and put them in that curry we had the night I died. I can't think of any other way. I'm not absolutely sure how but it was almost certainly my pills.'

Robert placed his guitar and bag by the front door and quietly made his way back to the living room. Gerald's computer was on and he was logged into Facebook. Robert looked over to her smiled, typed a short message on the laptop and pressed send. The rasping snores continued uninterrupted from the armchair. Shirley quietly studied Gerald and noticed that he'd put on a lot of weight. He really did look out for the count. She'd thought he was her knight in shining armour, picking her up from the depths of despair after Robert's dad had left her for a younger woman. He'd been so kind and attentive, but she realised now he'd had his own agenda and ambitions. The clues had all been there. He liked the best whisky, expensive cars, dining out and spent money at a rate far beyond his earnings. There was no point in dwelling on her lack of insight.

When Robert went to leave, she said, 'Be safe my lovely son. Have a wonderful life and know that you are loved so much.'

'Are you staying here, Mum? Why would you want to stay?'

'I think I should say good-bye to Gerald. Don't you?' she gave Robert a cheeky laugh.

'Yes,' he grinned. 'I may just take a gander through the window. At least he can't hurt you any more.'

The closing of the front door awakened Gerald.

He looked around him and took another swig of whisky. Shirley drifted around the room and hovered within his sight until he noticed her. She'd have rather been dressed up than in her pyjamas, but it didn't matter now. She wasn't trying to seduce him.

'What the devil!' he said.

'Good evening, Gerald, I guess you weren't expecting a visit from me.'

'How did you get in?'

'Through the window. It was actually quite easy. Are you missing me, Gerald? Shall I come and visit you every night?'

'You always were a troublesome bitch. This is my house now. You don't own anything anymore, do you? And dear lofty Robert is going to sign over control of his money to me tomorrow, which is a good thing. I won't have to get rid of him. He doesn't cost too much. He's normally off playing his bloody guitar with some band or other. Now why don't you go back where you belong. Get out of here,' he said grabbing the arm of the chair and trying to stand up.

'Now that's not very friendly. You promised to love me, but I guess that was all a lie. I'm such a bad judge of people. You just wanted my money. What a shame you didn't ask. I'd probably have given it to you.'

'Yes, you really are so stupid, but I'd still have been saddled with you and I wanted a fresh start; a chance to meet someone young and fit. Besides I didn't want to be grateful to you for the rest of my life. Thank you for the meal, darling. Thank you for the car,' he mimicked.

Thud, thud, thud, Shirley heard. It was the sound of the old man kicking his football. She knew her time in the house was running out.

A siren in the distance could be heard getting louder, and closer. It broke the total silence that only snow brings. Gerald rubbed his forehead as if he couldn't make sense of what was going on.

'Oh dear, have you got a headache? Too much whisky? Not enough home cooking?' asked Shirley in an ultra-sympathetic voice. 'How tiresome for you.'

'Just get lost,' Gerald muttered.

There was a loud pounding on the front door.

'I think that must be for you,' said Shirley. 'It could be the police. You see it would seem that you sent a message out, on Facebook, to all of our friends saying how you administered poison to your wife so that you could get your hands on her money. Confession is so good for the soul, don't you think Gerald? I'm so glad you owned up. I suspect the police will send somebody round to the back door as well, so you'd better let them in.'

At that moment the door flew open and Gerald found himself surrounded by police. At the same time Shirley found that a force was pulling her back towards the graveyard, but she didn't mind. Her son was safe and her husband would at last pay for snatching her precious years with her son. The sound of the wind swished by her, but it wasn't icy as it should have been.

'I miss you,' Robert shouted as she was pulled backwards through the air right by where he stood. She managed to blow him a kiss.

Shirley landed unceremoniously on the white ground near her headstone. The old man was still kicking the ball in a regular beat against his large marble stone.

'I took the liberty of bringing you back so you wouldn't be late,' he called over to her. 'You have to be back asleep before first light, or you'll be stuck here until someone rescues you. Believe me that's not a good thing.'

'I didn't know there was a time limit, but I sort of felt there would be. Thank you for looking out for me.'

'No worries. I'm guessing you managed to say

good-bye to your loved ones and sort out any outstanding affairs.'

'Yes. I think I did,' she smiled.

'You're the lucky one then. You'll be on your way to eternal life and freedom.'

'What about you?'

'I stayed out too long and I have to stay here until nature knows I am sorry for disregarding the rules and until someone rescues me.'

Knowing that she had no idea how to help this stranger she said, 'Oh you poor man,' as she reached out to put an arm round him. Surprisingly her arm didn't go through him and she could feel his sadness. All the years of his loneliness flitted through her mind and then the world wobbled and the two spirits flew to the stars in an instant.

There was no sign that anyone had been in the churchyard, except an old football that moved occasionally with the wind.

The Ghost of Love

'She lives her life in another world now,' I said to the doctor, as my auntie smiled with eyes that seemed to focus beyond the boundaries of the room.

He smiled at me and asked her some questions.

'Mrs Ash do you know who I am?' asked Dr Parsons.

My aunt smiled, 'Of course dear. Would you like a cup of tea?'

'No, thank you. Do you know what day of the week it is?'

'I don't need to know, dear. Weeks are a thing of the past. Can you see the poppies? Aren't they delicate; such big heads on tiny stems?'

I couldn't help but look out of the window. Snow carpeted the adjacent field and left a fringe along the top of the fence. Trees were covered in white lace. I shivered.

The doctor continued questioning gently, not showing any surprise at the random replies he received.

As he prepared to leave, he said to me, 'I'll refer your aunt to a specialist. It could take several weeks, but call me if you need me. She seems in good spirits and she's not showing any signs of pain.'

Suddenly auntie's eyes were focused. 'I won't see you again, Doctor. I'm off on my travels. Tonight, I'm spending with Susan. She's such a good girl. She's spent years looking after me and always with kindness. I want to say goodbye properly.'

The doctor gave me a sympathetic look, but as I saw him to the front door, he said, 'She's so believable, isn't she? It must make it very hard for you.'

We spent a lovely evening together, drinking tea and eating cake. Auntie reminisced about the past. We looked at sepia photographs and each held a story. I studied Auntie Moira and Uncle Walter's wedding photograph. They were so happy. Even now, when time had faded the image, you could see their joy. I'd never know a love like that, but I was not unhappy with my lot.

When she was ready for bed, she reached for me and gave me a hug.

'Goodnight, Susan. Be happy.'

'Goodnight,' I said as I switched off the light and quietly closed the door.

In the morning, I carried in her cup of tea, in her china cup with tiny roses. As soon as I opened the curtains, I knew she was gone. I touched her cold hand and saw the hint of a smile on her face. There was nothing anyone could do for her now. I was about to pick up the phone when I glanced out of the window. A sun light beam caught dust particles in its path, like dancing diamonds. I walked over to look at the view. The day would be full of formalities; it wouldn't hurt to take a moment to myself.

Outside, there was a young couple walking hand-in-hand, through a field of poppies, they turned, with bright smiles and waved. Immediately, I recognised them from their photograph. I waved right back, and as I did so, the scene changed to white. Snow covered the fields, lay delicately on the branches and collected into soft mounds under the fence.

Copper Head

It had always been my dream to go to art college, but I found that there were unkind people there, just like there were at school. Having an older sister, you'd assume would help, but it really didn't. I'm not sure why she didn't like me. She was so beautiful, there was no need for her to be jealous.

I was trying to look normal, carrying an overlarge rucksack full of art supplies, when three girls in my group started, calling out to me.

'Come to my place this evening, Copper Head. I'll lop off those crazy ginger curls and dye them black for you,' said Amanda.

'You have to admit your hair's out of control, don't you agree Verity?' chimed in Trudi.

'Yeah,' said Verity, not looking me in the face.

Nervously, I coughed and walked on. Then, I heard my sister.

'You really shouldn't mess with her. You've no idea who you're dealing with,' said Charlie.

It would be good to think she was defending me, but she wasn't. I turned the corner and entered the art block. Finding myself on my own, I settled down at the back of the class and set up for my final project. It was the examinable piece, which would be viewed by the course moderators. I was painting my version of the Lady of Shallot. It would be nothing like Waterhouse's version. She would be a modern girl, skimming down the river on a nifty canoe, wearing suitable sports gear. I decided I'd add my own symbolism as well. The canoe would have the Samaritans' number on the side, and there would be a bottle of anti-depressants, visible within the boat. I understood and had experienced the pain of unrequited love, although my 'would-be' love was no Knight of the Realm. He was a fellow student, who'd been happy to be with me, until he realized I was getting serious, and then he'd dumped me like a red-hot poker. I'd also decided that my river should have factories on the furthest side, spewing out dirty clouds of gas into the sky.

Having set up my canvass on one of the heavy wooden easels, I started to lay out my oils in true Bob Ross style.

At that moment, Verity walked in, looked all around her and came up to me.

'I'm sorry I was mean. You're strong. You can stand up to them. I can't. I love your copper curls.'

'Thanks,' I muttered and continued with my palette, as she scuttled away. Those copper curls were going to be the main warm colour in my desolate picture.

Amanda and Trudi walked in.

'Oh, here's Miss Goody Two Shoes. All set up and raring to go. Not sure why you're bothering. Your paintings are all weird,' said Amanda, and Trudi sniggered.

I couldn't think of a smart reply, so I coughed a couple of times and turned away. I ignored their comments and consulted my sketchbook, where I'd drafted out several compositions.

When the painting was finished, I carefully carried it home. I wasn't quite happy with it. Were the curls too bright? Was the hair too big and dominant in the picture? That weekend, I did another version in acrylics, with toned-down hair. I was sure this version would be more acceptable to my college mates and took it in to be displayed for the moderators.

We all painted our backing boards and hung our final pieces and then went round and viewed each other's. I loved seeing the variety of work around me. Some had done work inspired by Jackson Pollock, while others had done landscapes in the style of Monet.

'Good piece of work, Lillian, but you need a label with a title, your name and student number, preferably by the end of the day,' said the tutor. He was a kind man. Once or twice, he'd heard the trio being unkind and had intervened.

'Who forgot her label?' sneered Amanda. 'You needn't bother. It won't pass anyway. The whole point was, she was beautiful and her surroundings were beautiful.'

I went off to find a computer to make my label. Amanda might well be right but it was too late to change it now.

When I returned, the gallery was empty and the main light had been switched off. I liked the quiet. I wandered around and drank in the beautiful artwork. There were some talented students here. I paused by Philip's, longing to be with him again, but knowing I wouldn't. His painting was a powerful self-portrait, with just a hint of Lucian Freud's honesty.

When I found myself looking at my own picture, I pinned the label to the display board, before I noticed, the face had been slashed. Who would do something so malicious? I tried so hard not to be upset, but the anger and hurt welled up in me and was uncontrollable. I started coughing and couldn't stop. A lick of flame leapt from my mouth. I tried to hold my breath and made a run for the exit, but the more I tried to control my pain, the more fire shot through and out of my body. Soon, the room was filled with smoke, display boards were burning. I tried to rescue some of the paintings, but there wasn't time. There was chaos everywhere and then the sprinkler system activated and water showered down from the ceiling. There was nothing I could do. Nobody could know my secret or my chance of a normal life would be over. Only my family knew. They wouldn't tell anyone as they didn't want to be associated with my strangeness, but they'd made sure I moved out of their home, as soon as I could be independent.

I scurried out into the darkness and away from college. When I arrived at my rooms, I took a shower and shoved my clothes in the wash, so they wouldn't smell of smoke.

The next day, I decided to turn up as usual and be as shocked as the other students were going to be. All the art work was ruined and was being binned.

'This is an emergency,' said the tutor. 'The moderators will understand, but we still need to provide evidence of your work, so bring in your sketchbooks. Print out any photographs you took of your final pieces. The A3 printer will be reserved for this group today. Lillian, I believe you did a version in oils. Philip, I know you did several versions. Verity your drafts in your sketchbook will get you through. We may not be able to use the gallery but we'll set up in a couple of the empty classrooms. Off you go and see what you can find.'

We all went our separate ways, to collect other artwork, which we later set up on easels, with tables for our sketchbooks. My oil painting was praised by the moderators. In the end, I think it was actually better than the acrylic version, as the colours were more vivid and there was greater contrast, and of course it didn't have a slashed face.

Unfortunately, Amanda's was not commended, as she hadn't given enough thought to the use of colour. Such is life. I'm glad I'll not be with her again. As we left, the tutor called me over. He smiled and handed me a packet of cough sweets.

'I know what Amanda did to your picture, because I watched the CCTV footage and I know how the fire was started and that it was an accident. They'd call you Dragon Girl if they knew your secret, wouldn't they?' He smiled. 'I've spoken to Amanda and told her she's not welcome back to re-sit the year, next year. I can't officially punish her because I've destroyed the tape, so your secret is safe. Good luck with your future. I love the originality of your art.'

I thanked him and shook his hand. Sometimes, when you're born different, people who should love you, fail to, but others may show you kindness, when you least expect it.

The Apple Tree

The door creaked open slowly. Tanya felt the cold creep into every part of her body. The heating was on, but it made no difference. She pulled the woollen blanket up round her chin and noticed the air shimmering in front of her.

'Is there anyone there?' she called out in a frail voice.

There was silence.

'Who's there?' she called.

The silence extended its way into the room like the creeping tentacles of a vine. She looked at the shape appearing in front of her. The form was misty but vaguely familiar. She wished she didn't live by herself in this old draughty house, but she refused to be frightened. She'd always been strong.

'Who are you and what do you want?'

'I used to live here. My name is Thomas.'

'That's a good name. Well, Thomas, this is my house now and I'd like to know why you're here.'

'It's my home,' the small child replied. 'I've never left here.'

'I don't understand. What do you mean?'

'I lie beneath the apple tree in the garden. No-one ever blessed me or said a prayer. I can't leave because of how I died. I'm tied to this house.'

'Why have I never seen you before then?'

'That's what you always say,' said Thomas.

The image faded before Tanya's eyes and the room grew warmer.

'Hello, it's only me,' called Martha from the front door. 'How are we today? Oh, it's nice and warm in here.'

'Hello, who are you?' asked Tanya.

'It's me Martha. I've just bought you a nice hot meal. I come every day. Do you remember?'

'Hello Martha. What's for dinner today?'

'Macaroni cheese, followed by apple pie. Let me just get you some cutlery, and then I'll have to go. Lots of people waiting for their dinner.'

When Martha closed the door, Tanya settled down and ate her meal. She had just finished when the door creaked slowly and Tanya felt the cold again. A little boy appeared before her out of a mist. She held the blanket close to her.

'Who are you?' she asked.

'My name is Thomas. When I was alive, I lived here. Now I lie under the apple tree in the garden and I can't leave because of how I was killed.'

'Well Thomas, this is my house now. I think you're making me very cold.'

'I'm cold. I've been cold for sixty-five years.'

'What can I do to help you to leave?'

'You can say a prayer about how sorry you are that I died such a violent death.'

'Well, of course I'm sorry. No-one should die a violent death. Let me go and get my coat and I'll come into the garden with you.'

Tanya went out of the room to get her coat, but when she got to the hall, she couldn't remember what she'd gone to collect. She went back to sit by the fire and pulled the blanket round her. The soft texture was comforting, but there was a chill in the air. A young boy appeared before her.

'Who are you?' she asked.

'My name is Thomas. You were going to get your coat and come into the garden and say a prayer for me about how sorry you were that I died young.'

'Was I? Well Thomas why would I do that?'

'So, I don't make you cold anymore.'

'That's a good reason.' Tanya picked up her pen and notebook.

She wrote, 'Get coat. Go into the garden. Say prayer for Thomas, so he doesn't make me cold anymore.'

Then she stood up holding her notebook. When she reached the hall, she put on her coat and went back to her chair and put down the notebook. She headed for the garden, following Thomas but when she opened the back door, she couldn't think why she was going into the garden and turned round and went back to her chair. Tanya snuggled under the warm woollen blanket. She was very cold. She picked up her notebook and read: Get coat. Go into the garden. Say prayer for Thomas so he doesn't make me cold any more. Then she looked up and saw a young boy.

'You must be Thomas. Can I say the prayer here?'

Thomas looked at her sadly. 'If you like.'

Tanya was not a religious person, but there could be no harm in saying a prayer.

'Dear World, I'm sorry that this poor boy, Thomas was killed violently and is now buried under my apple tree. Please let him go where he should be, so my house won't be cold anymore.'

Thomas sighed and went out and lay under the apple tree again. He was weary having to explain the same thing over and over again, and he knew that 'prayer' wouldn't work, because there was no genuine feeling in it.

The door creaked slowly. Tanya felt the cold creep into every part of her body. The heating was on, but it made no difference. Her thick fluffy blanket felt like the inside of a freezer. Nothing she did made her warm.

When Martha arrived the next day, it was to find Tanya stiff and as cold as a block of ice. While

Martha waited for the ambulance, she felt a severe chill enter her bones and then a small boy appeared before her. For some reason she wasn't frightened and then he started speaking.

'My mother killed me when I was eight, but she could never be sorry about it because she lost her mind and memory.'

'Who was your mother, Thomas?'

The little boy pointed at Tanya. Martha said nothing, but opened her arms to hold the child. He went straight to her.

'I'm so sorry Thomas,' she said. 'I'm sure she would've been sorry, if she'd remembered. Perhaps that's why she lost her memory.'

She felt a strong hug and then he was gone. Sun started streaming in through the windows. A ray of light danced onto the mantelpiece and struck an old photograph that Martha had never noticed before. It showed a young boy. He was smiling.

Elizabeth

To this day I can't remember why I was walking through the graveyard. The moon cast a half light and the cold seeped through my clothes. The graveyard could have been a setting for a Dicken's novel.

At first, I heard a faint cry, but as I listened, I was drawn to the eerie sound. The crying became heart wrenching and then a small child appeared, crouched by a stone angel. Her hair was long and lank and she had huge, sad eyes. She pulled the rags she wore closely to her. My heart welled up with pity that, in this day and age, any child should be in such poverty and on their own at night.

'What's wrong? Can I help you?' I asked.

'I've lost my way and can't find my mother,' she said.

'Where were you going, child?'

'That's the worst thing, Sir, I can't remember.'

I tried to think of the last time anyone had called me, Sir. For some reason it made me feel uncomfortable, but this was still a child in trouble. I reached for my phone to call the police.

'Oh, please don't worry about me, Sir. I'll just look down this row and see if I can find Mama.'

I put my phone away. Perhaps she was frightened of the police, but if we didn't find her mother in half an hour, I would call them. As we walked, I tried to work out how old she was. She was tiny and yet she held herself so proudly and there was something about her that was, what I'd call, mature.

'What's your name?' I asked.

'Elizabeth, Sir, Elizabeth Derby.'

This was no ordinary child. Her skin was almost white and her torn garments a murky grey, as if they'd never seen a washing machine. There was a chill in the air around her and as I peered through the darkness, I realized that her clothes were from a century ago. Was I was talking to a ghost or was this some sort of party trick? Yet she was still a child and she looked so lost. How could I abandon her until she'd found her mother? I decided to ask her directly if she was a ghost.

'Were you looking for your grave, Elizabeth?' I said gently.

'No, I'm looking for my mother, Margaret Derby, Sir.'

So, I wandered through the graveyard with this ghost child, searching for Margaret Derby and while she looked for her mother, I read the names on the grave stones, but I saw no Elizabeth or Margaret Derby.

The churchyard contained rows of graves and as we finished looking in one row, another row seemed to appear through the mist. I realize now that I'd lost all sense of time. I was mesmerized with the task of returning this child to her mother. The cold seemed to ebb away as we continued to walk.

'You should leave me, Sir. I will find Mama in time.'

But I couldn't leave this child with the sad eyes, that looked at me and held my attention, as if she'd reached in and touched my soul.

The graves all started to merge into one image, although I knew that some were upright and others tilted. Some had modern headstones and others were covered in moss. The statues and angels swirled around me and the pathways converged.

'You are kind,' said Elizabeth, 'but you should go back to your life.'

'I'd just like to see you with your mother,' I said.

Her round eyes looked moist.

Eventually, she sighed and said, 'I must rest,' so we sat down by a magnificent, ancient Yew Tree. She leaned against me, but there was no pressure on my arm, just a piercing cold, that shot through my body.

She was so small and elf like. I couldn't move and disturb her.

Elizabeth closed her eyes and I sat there quietly contemplating what I should do. I was certain now that this child was from the past, so calling the police was not an option. If I called and said that I was sitting in a graveyard, with a ghost child, who'd lost her mother, the police would either come and take me off to a mental hospital, or would ignore the call completely. I looked down at Elizabeth and thought that I could sit here for a while, until she awoke. I was a young, fit man and although I was cold, I was wearing a coat. The graveyard had ceased to seem eerie as I had Elizabeth to keep me company. I don't know how long I sat there, before I fell asleep, but I remember feeling calm.

When I woke, it was to a different world. Elizabeth was gone. I was no longer sitting by the ancient Yew. I was viewing the graveyard from above. There was the sound of birdsong and a clear blue sky. The sun was warm on my back. It took me a moment to realize that I was floating in mid-air. I looked below and saw the graveyard in sunlight, which covered only about an acre of land, yet we had walked along row upon row of graves the previous night. Surely it had been a much bigger place then?

I should have listened to Elizabeth. She'd told me, more than once to leave her. She was like a reluctant mermaid, drawing unsuspecting sailors to their death. I felt that Elizabeth had known what she was doing, even though she'd seemed to be a reluctant participant. I wondered how she'd come to her fate. Was it a punishment for some misdemeanour during her lifetime? I hoped that one day she'd be allowed to rest with her mother.

A gentle breeze brought me out of my pondering. I would never go home again, or see my family. I wouldn't become the famous author I'd worked so hard to be, and there in a corner of the graveyard was my body, propped up against the ancient Yew Tree, like an awkward mannequin.

Chantal

Working in the remote, high-tech laboratories just outside Inverness, Chantal Lyon was a quiet, but valued member of the community. She was a bit of an enigma to the other researchers, as she often went off on her own and yet she wasn't unsociable. She knew the right things to say to cheer people up or to give encouragement, but she didn't go out partying and nobody had ever seen her drunk. She wasn't quite beautiful as she had a strong jaw line but her eyes were large and deep and held attention. She wore bright red lipstick which matched her immaculate nails and her shapely legs were set off well in high thin stilettos.

Chantal had grown up following in her father's scientific footsteps, although she'd never known her father. He'd died before she was born. He was doing research into DNA and using cross human-animal embryos, to see if there was any way to control Alzheimer's, in an aging population. Although slightly unorthodox, he was liked well enough by his colleagues and adored by women. When his body was found, it was thought to have been mauled by a wild panther, so it hit the National news headlines.

There was little evidence, although lots of rumours, that there were wild panthers in Scotland. Several people claimed to have seen them, but the few photographs that had been produced were inconclusive. However, the coroner found that the injuries to Doctor Lyon were consistent with those of being mauled by a large creature.

Chantal's mother had died giving birth, and so Chantal had been brought up, without love or affection, by an aunt who'd felt it her duty to care for this orphaned member of the family. In spite of this background, Chantal grew up and thrived. She was a high achieving scientist in her own right by the time she was twenty-eight.

The director of the research institute informed his staff that they must attend a government briefing on Saturday in Fort William's town hall and her colleague Simon Fortesque offered to drive Chantal. He was a tall, dark and good looking man, who'd never shown any interest in the women at the research centre, but was well known for his inappropriate and often inebriated behaviour in Inverness. This wasn't something that was held against him by the locals, as being able to have a good drink was an acceptable part of life these days.

Chantal hoped to be home by six in the evening, but she couldn't get Simon away from the buffet that was served after the meeting. Finally, they got into the car. It was quite a way into the journey that Simon, forgetting that he never mixed work and women, made a very clumsy pass at Chantal. She could feel the blood boil under her skin and knew the dangers she risked.

'Stop the car,' she demanded. 'I want to get out now.'

'You can't. We're in the middle of nowhere and it's getting dark,' he said. 'Look I'm sorry I made that suggestion. I promise I won't touch you.'

'I said, *stop the car*.'

Simon gave in and pulled the car onto the side of the road. Normally he didn't have this effect on women and even though he'd been rejected, he felt uneasy about letting her out on her own in the middle of nowhere. He tried one last time, 'Look just let me drop you off in Inverness.'

Chantal ignored him. She swung the car door open and elegantly climbed out of the low seat. When he turned to look at her as he drove away, she was gone. It was as if she'd vaporized into the twilight.

It wasn't until Simon was getting out of his car at his home that he noticed the passenger seat had been ripped. *Bitch*, he thought, *she'll pay for that*.

Meanwhile Chantal was walking along the completely deserted road. All her senses were heightened. The utter loneliness of the place struck her. The light of the day was almost gone and there were no street lamps. She was pleased that there was light from the full moon. It struck her that she really was miles from anywhere and it was going to be a long night. Maybe she should've stayed in Simon's car, but she couldn't be too careful.

A haunting screeching sound from a fox broke the silence and startled her, but she took a deep breath and carried on. She could smell the freshness of the night. This was no different from all the other trials she'd had to face in her life. She just had to get on with it. The road was leading through a thick dark wood, which held many moving shadows. Fleetingly she wondered about her father. *Had it been in this sort of countryside that he'd died? Had he been trying to trap a panther?*

There was a rustling of leaves and the sound of soft footfalls. By now the adrenaline was racing around Chantal's body. Her eyes glittered in the darkness and she increased her walking pace.

The fox again called in the night and Chantal clearly heard twigs crunch in the shadowy undergrowth. She ran her hands through her sleek black hair and tried to make her breath even. She was going to get through this night.

After two more miles, Chantal discarded her shoes. She found that walking on the road, barefoot was actually quite comfortable and certainly she could move much more quickly. Suddenly standing before her was a large black cat. It certainly wasn't a domestic cat. *So this is how it would be,* she thought, *miles from anywhere, just like my father*. Not knowing whether to run but realizing even if she could make it up a tree, so would the cat, she stood still and stared at him. She recognised his beauty, even as she recognised his power. They both stood still and stared. There was no way out, but suddenly he moved, stealthily and slowly and skirted around her, always keeping his eyes on her. Then he was gone.

Chantal only started to move when she could see him no more. She drew herself up to her full height and quickly marched onwards. *Perhaps he'd recently eaten,* she thought.

There were no cars driving past and gradually Chantal relaxed into the night. She was pleased with her fitness and knew that she could walk all night long. In the distance she heard the rumble of a car's engine. Her senses became alert. Should she flag down the car or dive for the cover of the woods? The car was slowing and she could see the silhouette of a woman. She wasn't going to get in this woman's car. Why would a woman alone stop and offer a stranger a lift? No, she would trust her instincts.

The woman looked out of the window and said, 'Do you need a lift?'

'Do I look like I need a lift?' Chantal hissed aggressively. The woman stepped on the accelerator and shot off.

Chantal knew she'd made the right decision, especially when three miles later, she came across a parked lorry. She felt the adrenaline surge and all her senses prickle. She could hear every little noise as she crept up and peeked through the cab window.

The driver was fast asleep in a hammock type bed, totally oblivious to being spied upon. Chantal stepped down again, slipped off her T- shirt and hid it under a tree and went back to the cab door and banged loudly.

Her heart was thumping hard in her chest, and she could feel the blood rushing through her brain.

When the driver opened the door, she said, 'Can you help me with this? I need you to take a look.'

The driver eagerly leapt down from the cab. She smiled. It wouldn't hurt to play with him a bit, as she beckoned him towards the woods. She leaned forward as if to kiss him, and then the attack began. She sank her teeth into his neck, and her hands with their long lacquered nails, sunk into his flesh. He was no match for her, although he fought for a while. Her powerful jaw ripped at his throat and the blood spurted and dribbled and oozed.

The driver's look of surprise was lost on Chantal as she was immersed in her own world. Suddenly, as if by some unexplained charm it started to pour with rain and she threw back her head and embraced the wetness. She left the carcass in the grass, by the road, and out of the corner of her eye, she noticed a dark shadow take over where she'd left off.

The rain washed away all the crimson debris and she picked up her T-shirt from under the tree and climbed into the cab.

Leaving the nameless driver and his shadowy companion, she drove the lorry to the outskirts of Inverness, where she set it alight.

'Morning,' she said brightly to Simon as she passed his desk. He'd been going to tackle her about his car seat, but something about her stopped him. He'd just read how a man had been found, mauled and half eaten, on the road he'd left her on last night. She was looking sleek and alert. Her black hair shining and smooth and he noticed for the first time how well she moved.

'Morning, you got back okay, I see.'

'Oh yes, it was fine.' She smiled. She could smell his fear.

Chantal sat down in her office. She'd often wondered why her aunt had never loved her, but she was beginning to understand. Of course, there was no doubt that she was human, but she realized that her humanness had been enhanced, probably by her father, as one of his own private experiments. She had her father's brains and enough femininity from her mother to make her attractive. Chantal knew she also had reason and choices. These were signs that she was part of the human race. Her mother had died in childbirth because she, the baby was not just a normal baby. She must get hold of her father's notes from the archives. She knew that there were times in the past when she'd had difficulty in stopping herself killing things, but last night she'd been in control. She'd not killed her colleague, which would have caused a lot of questions. She'd not dived into a stranger's car. She'd waited until the time was right and she could set up the kill. The scientist in her, thought about trying to find ways to curtail her urges, but she knew now that she could control it. She'd suppressed her needs for so long, and now she was beginning to like who she was. She'd probably get away with it, as long as she only indulged herself occasionally.

This story was first published in the anthology, Missing.

Witch Hunt

I could smell food cooking close by. My stomach responded to the aroma. After days of just water and stale biscuits, I longed for something tasty. Automatically, I walked faster. As I turned the corner, I saw an old man sitting by a fire roasting some meat; probably rabbit. He was big and bald and although his back was slightly bent, he didn't look to be past his strength. Nervously, I walked towards him, wondering if he'd be friendly. I certainly didn't want any trouble. He heard my footsteps and turned towards me.

'Don't suppose you've enough to share?' I called, stopping where I was. I didn't want to look as if I'd grab his food and run.

He looked me up and down and then smiled. 'There's plenty of food, if you're on your own. Come and join me.'

I dumped my bag by the fire and sat on my black cloak. Brushing my long dark hair away from my face I let the flames warm me. It was the most wonderful feeling. Soon, the meal was ready. I cannot describe how delicious the food was. I wiped the juices away from my chin, with my hand and picked up the mug of strong black tea. It was not to my taste but I didn't want to offend my guest.

'So, why is a pretty young thing like you wandering around here, on your own, at this time of night,' he asked.

'I'm Topaz. I live in Bycross Mill, in the valley beyond and I'm travelling to see my grandmother. She lives in Wootten Stanley. Somehow, I seem to have taken a wrong turn and I don't recognise the landscape. I don't suppose you have a map.'

He took out a small map, made from a lined backed material and placed it on the ground before me. He pointed first to Bycross Mill and then to Wootten Stanley. Then, he showed me where we were. Past Wootten Stanley

You're miles out of your way. It would be dangerous to travel tonight. You'd better stay here, by the fire, until the morning.'

'So, why are you here?' I asked'

He looked at me closely. 'You're looking tired,' he said. 'Lay down by the fire and I'll tell you who I am.'

He looked a kind man and he'd just fed me and offered me a place to rest for the night, so I spread out my cloak and lay down. He didn't move. The fire lent its rosy glow and I felt safe.

'My name is Volt Hunter. I'm hunter by name and by profession. I hunt witches and deliver them to the authorities.'

Fear spread through me and chilled my bones. I sat up slowly and schooled my voice to be calm.

'So, you believe in witches, do you? I don't. Are you telling me you've actually met a real witch?'

'Who knows?' he smiled. 'I get paid for delivering them to the authorities and that's the end of my job. Do you know there's a witch on the run from Wootten Stanley at the moment? Let me show you her poster.'

He leaned over and passed me the poster. There in front of me was a drawing of my likeness. I handed it back to him.

'Poor woman. She'll die a most excruciating death. I'm glad you know I'm not a witch.'

'Now, how do I know that Topaz?"

"Well, it's obvious. I approached you for food. A witch wouldn't need to do that. A witch, if such beings exist, would be able to catch their own food; light their own fire. That's what they do, isn't it?'

He smiled. 'I think you're missing the point, dear girl. I just have to deliver someone who looks like the poster and I get paid. You'll do, whether or not you're a witch.'

'So, what happens now? Do you tie me up and hall me back to the village in the middle of the night?'

'No, Topaz. You lie down again and you'll sleep. Your tea was drugged. You can be comfortable tonight. Tomorrow when we're both rested, I'll take you to the village. It can be as easy or as hard as you like.'

'Don't you care what they'll do to me? And what about my grandmother? How can you condemn me to a death by drowning or by fire? Doesn't it prey on your conscience? Do you have no concept of good and evil?'

'Lie down NOW, Topaz. I have to eat just like the next man. I've never killed any woman, witch or otherwise. If you really want to know what I think, I'll tell you.'

I lay back down on my cloak.

'Yes, I really want to know.'

'Obviously, there's no such thing as witches. These poor creatures have just annoyed someone powerful, but that's their problem, not mine. I don't commit the murder. It's not my responsibility. In your case, I think it's a terrible waste to kill someone so beautiful and young, but that's mankind for you. Now go to sleep.'

He got out a rug and lay down on the other side of the fire. Soon his snores could be heard rattling into the night. I sat up slowly and then stood up, quietly lifting my cloak from the ground. I wrapped it round myself. How lucky I had poured the tea into the ground behind me. It had smelt foul. I looked over at Volt Hunter and silently swore he would never cause another woman to die a terrifying death.

In the morning, a tiny mouse woke up on the rug by the dying fire. I was walking in the fresh sunshine, listening to the birds. I laughed at the thought of how many predators there are for mice. He would be hunted every day of his life, be it a short one or a long one.

This story was first published in the anthology, The Mermaid.

Dare

As Sheila and Donna, walked home from school in the dark, Sheila's brain was filtering all the information she could muster. Suddenly today, Donna had decided to become her friend. Donna, who was popular with the boys, wore all the latest clothes and had loads of friends. Mostly Donna's gang just left her alone. She was boring; worked hard and did what her parents told her. She didn't have a boyfriend, hardly ever wore make up and didn't drink. Sheila did have a couple of close friends, but she knew that it wasn't wise to upset Donna, so she'd gone along with the strange new friendship. In spite of all their differences, they had a similar look about them. Sheila wore her blonde hair in a single plait down her back, while Donna's was loose. They were about the same height and could have been taken for sisters.

'I'll see you tomorrow, Donna. I don't go that way. It takes you through the churchyard,' said Sheila.

'Don't be such a chicken. We can both go this way and then I can get to my house and you can cut through the churchyard. It'll be quicker for you and we can spend more time together.'

'Sorry, I'm going the other way.'

'You're never frightened of ghosts, are you? I thought someone as clever as you, would know that's all rubbish. Go on, I dare you to go through the churchyard'

'No, I'm sure it's all rubbish. It's people alive and well, that frighten me. See you,' she called over her shoulder, as she quickly marched away.

Donna called out after her, 'Come back, I'll walk through the churchyard with you.'

'Sorry, see you tomorrow.'

She was not her father's daughter for nothing. He'd taught her well, being an inspector in the local police force. He'd told her, never to go into the graveyard on her own, as drug dealers hung out there sometimes, and they'd see her as a potential money source. He'd also drummed into her to trust her instincts and that if she was feeling uncomfortable with someone, to get away. She was definitely feeling uncomfortable with Donna. She couldn't understand why Donna wanted her to go into the graveyard. What was going on? She looked back but Donna was gone, so she ran home. It had been a very strange day.

At eleven that night, the front doorbell rang. Inspector Willis, one of her dad's friends, stood in the doorway.

'Can we speak to Sheila please?' he asked and so she came downstairs in her sensible pyjamas, wrapped up in a warm dressing gown.

'You can talk to me on my own. At sixteen, I'm sure your dad wouldn't mind,' he said.

'No, I haven't done anything wrong. He might as well be here.'

Her father sat on the sofa with her as Terry Willis asked her questions.

'Can you tell me about your day?'

'Well yes, but there's nothing that will interest you.'

'We're particularly interested in any contact you've had with Donna Lane.'

'Okay, I see. Usually, Donna sticks with her group of friends, but today for some reason she wanted to be my friend. I don't know why, but I went along with it, because I know what she can do if you upset her.'

'Did she ask you for anything, money, jewellery, your phone...?'

'No, but she insisted we walk home together, which I didn't really want to do, but as I said, you don't want to upset her. I always walk through the town, because it's lighter and there are people around, but when we came to Church Walk, she wanted us to go up there. I said, no and she said, I was scared. I said, 'See you' and marched off. I'm not allowed to go through the churchyard.'

'And you always do what your dad says?'

Sheila smiled. 'He told me about the drug dealers that work there and that seemed a good reason not to go there, besides I felt Donna was trying to manipulate me. I didn't feel that the friendship was real.'

Her dad, who'd kept quiet during the questioning, now asked the obvious question?'

'Has something happened to Donna, Terry?'

'I'm sorry to have to tell you that she was bludgeoned to death.' Her body was found in the churchyard and you Sheila, are the last person to see her alive.

'Except the murderer,' said Sheila.

A week later, Sheila was standing at the entrance to Church Walk.

'You don't have to do this if you don't want to,' her dad said.

'No, I will. We need to find out what happened.'

'Okay,' said Inspector Willis. 'You're going to pretend to be Donna. For some reason she decided to enter the churchyard, even though that was not her direct route home. There are three of our officers already in the churchyard. Your dad will walk about twenty paces behind you and there are officers at both ends of the path. You're all wired up, so just shout if anyone approaches you. We'll be filming the whole reconstruction from the church tower and we'll put it on the local TV, tomorrow night. Any questions?'

'No, let's just get it done.'

'When you're ready,' said Inspector Willis.

Sheila took a deep breath and started walking up Church Walk. It was dark and the street lights cast small pools of yellow against the pavement. As she entered the churchyard, the darkness deepened. There were no overhead lights. Sheila could feel her heartbeat quicken. Her eyes darted across the graveyard. She could dimly make out the large stones that were jutting out at assorted angles. These were the old graves. There was complete quiet. She listened for her dad's footsteps, but heard none.

Suddenly, she heard a girl shouting out. She held her breath. 'It's me, she wouldn't come. Dylan, I tried, but she wouldn't come. Dylan where are you? Arrrrgh. Dylan it's me.'

Sheila stood absolutely still and turned round to look where the voice was coming from. She was just in time to see Donna being hit on the head by a shadowy figure and fall to the ground. What was going on? Donna had been dead a week.

Then she heard running feet coming towards her. Her dad was shouting.

'What's wrong? Why have you stopped? Did you see something?'

'Something spooked me, but I'm all right now. Did anyone hear anything?'

Her dad checked, but none of the officers had heard a noise.

'Do you want me to go on?'

'Yes, if you're up to it, but I'm going to be right behind you,' her dad said.

When they reached the end of the churchyard, Inspector Willis was there to greet them. He was scanning through the digital video.

'Okay, what happened? Did you see something? Did you remember something?' Inspector Willis asked.

Sheila knew that if she said she'd seen Donna, everyone would think she'd gone mad, but she was sure of what she'd seen. Donna had tried to persuade her to go through the churchyard, where Dylan was going to attack her. But why? She knew that somehow she needed to direct the police to Dylan Marsh. She was sure it had been him who'd killed Donna.

'I'd like to go home. I'm sorry I messed up tonight but I think Donna was setting me up to be attacked. I just don't know why. Have you questioned Dylan Marsh?'

Her dad and Inspector Willis exchanged a meaningful glance.

'Why do you mention him, love?' asked her dad.

'No reason really, except I caught him looking at me with absolute hatred on the day Donna died. I remembered his look while I was walking. It's probably just my imagination though, because I haven't done anything to annoy him.'

'Come on Sheila, let's get you home,' her dad said putting his arm round her.

When the police searched Dylan Marsh's home, they found nothing at first and then Inspector Willis asked to look at his leather coat. It turned out that he'd wiped it down with a damp cloth but he hadn't thrown it away, because it was his favourite and he couldn't afford a new one. With forensic evidence against him, he confessed to killing Donna.

'It should've been that bitch, Sheila. Her dad put my dad away. I was going to make him pay. Why should he have his family when mine is blown to bits? I was going to make him suffer, but I'm sorry I did Donna. She was my mate,' he spat out at Inspector Willis, as he was being led away.

'I don't know how you knew it was Dylan, but we might not have got there without your input. Sorry my job put you in danger,' her dad said to her later.

'Well, it was also your job that saved my life. Anyway, I don't think I'll ever go in that churchyard again,' Sheila said with a smile.

But the girl in the churchyard continued to shout and was sometimes seen by people passing by. Some believe that those who die a violent death, can leave an imprint on this earth, like an old-fashioned video recording, which plays again and again.

This story was first published in the anthology, Pebble on the Beach.

Angel in Our Midst

Star Seint stumbled into the fast-food store. She was exhausted having worked at the children's hospice for four hours. Young Tony's leukaemia would go now, but the effort had drained Star to the point of exhaustion.

'Chips, double portion and a coffee please,' she said, and as she spoke, she heard, 'Chips, double portion, and a coffee please,' from the adjacent queue. At first, she thought that someone was mimicking her, but as she looked over at the tall, thin, man with black eyes, she realized he was not even aware of her. Star was not surprised. She was washed out, a pale shadow of what she could be, but it would all be worth it, if seven year old Tony, lived. Even at her best she was not a beauty. Her eyes slanted slightly upwards and her face was too thin. Her mousy hair was pulled off her face in an untidy pony tail.

Making her way over to an empty table she slumped into a chair. The thin, dark-haired man came over.

'May I join you? You obviously made a good choice about food,' he smiled and his face lost its harshness.

'Please do. I won't be very good company though, I'm afraid I'm exhausted.'

'Yes, you do look pale. Believe it or not, I'm a doctor - Doctor Gerald Parker. Are you unwell?'

'I'm fine, just been working hard. I'm Star Seint.'

'Well Star, it's not good to work to the point of exhaustion,' he said, as he covered his chips with salt and vinegar. 'So, what do you do?'

This was always tricky to answer. 'I volunteer at a number of medical establishments and offer therapies, that make people who are seriously ill, feel better.'

'That sounds very altruistic. You don't charge fees or claim miracle cures?'

'I never claim cures and my work is entirely voluntary. Where do you work?'

'St Mark's General Hospital, mostly. When I've finished here, I'm going back there to finish my paper work. Thursdays and Fridays I run a private practice in Haslemere Street.'

Star felt an itch in her back and wriggled. She quickly finished her chips and downed her coffee. 'Must be off. It was good to meet you, Doctor Parker.'

'Gerald, please,' he called after her, but she'd gone.

Outside, there was a white mist, making visibility of more than a few feet, impossible. Star checked no-one was looking and shook out her wings. With speed and grace, she flew to the top of the cathedral. It was such a release to fly. Folding wings for hours on end wasn't very comfortable. She slipped through a gap under the roof and made her way to her hammock and there she slept the sound sleep of the innocent.

Gerald trudged back to the hospital. It was rare that a girl walked away from him and he found he couldn't get Star out of his head. There was something different about her. He'd felt content in her presence, which was most unusual. When had he last felt so calm in anyone's company? He couldn't remember. At work, he strived to impress. It was an inborn instinct. He didn't want to live in the gutter as his father had done. His father had been a drunk, while he was a dedicated doctor. He was proud that his patients received the best care. He strove for perfection and those who worked for him knew, they had to meet his high standards, or they'd be moved on. Tonight, he would finish his paperwork and then research the skin condition that one of his patients was suffering from.

The following day, on his rounds, he stopped to talk to Mrs Higgins, who had the skin complaint. She was reiterating all of the symptoms, which he already knew, having studied her file in depth. Feeling rather irritated, he opened his mouth to speak, when a sense of calm washed over him. Gerald turned round and there quietly standing in the doorway was Star.

He smiled, 'Have you come to see me?'

'No, Doctor Parker. I came to speak with Mrs Higgins.'

'Excuse me, then,' he said and left the room.

Later that day, he went back to speak to Mrs Higgins.

'Such a lovely lady,' she said. 'Never met her before and don't know why she chose to come and chat to me, but she held my hand and told me the itchiness would go and then the rashes would heal.'

'That'll be the steroid cream working, then,' said Gerald.

'Oh yes, of course, Doctor.'

The next day he discovered that Mrs Higgins was completely free from her skin condition. It was miraculous. Although most surprised at the speed of her recovery, he handed her a feedback form and discharged her from hospital.

Over the next week, three more of his patients had unexpected cures and he discovered that each one had been visited quietly and unobtrusively by Star. He must speak to her. If she had a gift, he would offer her a job in his private clinic and make a fortune – as well as help a lot of sick people.

Star flew over the city. It was twilight and no-one was looking upwards. She was listening for cries of help. It was a coincidence that four of Dr Gerald Parker's patients had called out for help, just after she'd met him. Or was it? The truth was he was very good looking and she was drawn to him, but no good ever came from angels trying to be friends with mortals. In fact, she'd been strongly warned against it by her parents. She had to face the fact that on Earth she was a freak and if anyone discovered she was an angel, they would probably lock her up and examine her, perhaps even dissect her. She shuddered. There was no way to hide wings if you were intimate with someone, so you just had to keep away.

'Chips' she thought. If she couldn't have a special friend, then she'd have a plate of chips, so she made her way towards the ground.

Holding a large plate of chips and a coffee she walked over to a table and realized that Dr Parker was sitting nearby. 'It wouldn't hurt just to talk,' she thought and went over to him.

'I was hoping to see you, Star. You're looking much better today.'

'Thank you,' she smiled.

Gerald told her that he'd noticed how she'd helped his patients and offered her a job.

'I'm really honoured but that's not how I work.'

'But everyone must make a living.'

'I'm sorry, but I wish you success in your business.'

'My business is making people well,' he raised his voice but Star said goodnight and left.

A year passed. Star continued to quietly heal people who called for her help. Occasionally, she and Gerald bumped into each other. She knew that Gerald was now recognised as one of the best doctors in the area. He ran a private clinic and opened a practice in Harley Street. At St Mark's, he became one of the highest paid consultants. And then a terrible thing happened. One night, she flew too close to the nest of a Peregrine Falcon. The bird viciously attacked her and tore her left wing. Star managed to gain the sanctuary of her hammock in the cathedral. She curled up in pain but there was nothing she could do to heal herself. If the bird had attacked her skin, she could have mended the wound, but she couldn't repair her wing. The next day was worse. She had a fever and was shivering. She had to get help. It took her two hours to make her way to Gerald's clinic, but it was early in the morning and no-one was about. She saw his car draw up. Creeping out from the shadows, she called to him.

'Gerald, I need your help.'

She felt herself lifted and carried into his consulting room.

'Now tell me what happened,' he spoke kindly.

'I'm not what I seem,' she started. 'On my back I have wings. One is torn. It needs to be sewn to be mended. Please help me.'

'Is this a joke? Do you think I haven't got better things to do...?' As he spoke, she removed her top and turned her back towards him. There was silence.

'Is it painful?' he asked.

'Very.'

'You probably need an anaesthetic,' he said. She sighed. He was going to examine her. He might lock her up. She would be worth a fortune to him.

'But as you're not human, I've no idea what that would do to you. All I can do is sew your wing together. It will hurt. Let's get on and get it done, shall we?' He went over to the sink and scrubbed his hands.

As he worked, he realized that he could use his knowledge about her wings to blackmail her into working for him. His already successful clinic would become world famous, if he could guarantee a cure for any ailment. But she was so tiny and fragile and she'd trusted him. Her wings felt like silk. He understood immediately the risk she'd taken in coming to him. He thought how she spent her life tirelessly helping others. He thought about all of the patients she'd helped and never once taken the credit. He could hear her muted sobs as each time he sewed a stitch it caused her pain, but he had to do many small stitches if her wing was to hold together. When he finished, he asked her to stretch her wings but she could hardly move the broken one.

'I'm going to take you to my home, so you can rest properly. You're not to do any work until you heal. Promise.'

All day she slept and as evening came, she stepped from the bed and stretched her wings. They spread out and she flew carefully round the room. 'I must test them properly,' she thought and opened the window. The air felt cool and fresh and her fever was gone. She flew up to the cathedral and then back through the window to his flat. He was standing there with take-away chips and coffee, looking sad.

'I thought you'd gone,' he said.

'Not without saying thank you,' she leaned upwards and kissed him. 'I can fly again. You're the best doctor in the world.'

Doctor Gerald Parker knew that he didn't need to prove himself anymore. There was only one person's opinion that mattered – and she was standing beside him.

If you've enjoyed this book, you might enjoy other books by Penny Luker.

Missing - *Short stories for adults*
Pebble on the Beach – *Short stories for adults*
The Mermaid - *Short stories for adults*
Lady in the Woods - *Short stories for adults*

The Truth Finder - *Fantasy novels*
The Visualizer
The Healer

Nature's Gold - *Poetry*
Autumn Gold - *Poetry*
Shadows of Love - *Poetry*

Children's Books

The Green Book *a gentle, magical story*
Chapter book
Tiny Tyrannosaurus *a gentle, magical story*
Chapter book
Pablo the storytelling bear, *a magical story*
Chapter book
Desdemona. The dragon without any friends.
Picture book

Read more of Penny Luker's writing at:

www.pennyluker.wordpress.com

Printed in Great Britain
by Amazon

71898741R00047